The Mystery of Mapplesham Market

By Linda Newbery

illustrated by Paul Hampson and Fred van Deelen

Contents

PEARSON
Longman

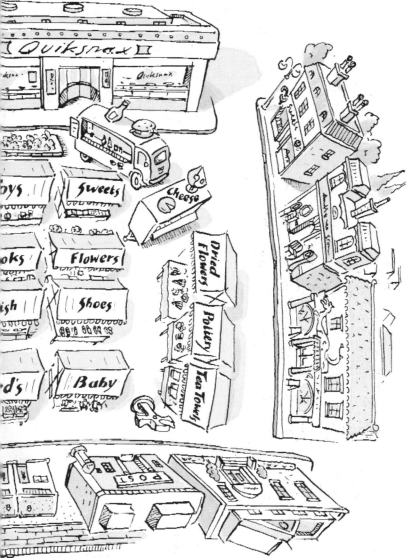

Text © Linda Newbery 2004
Series editors: Martin Coles and Christine Hall

PEARSON EDUCATION LIMITED
Edinburgh Gate
Harlow
Essex CM20 2JE
England

www.longman.co.uk

First published 2004

ISBN 0582 79629 6

Illustrated by Paul Hampson and Fred van Deelen (The Organisation)

Printed in Great Britain by Scotprint, Haddington

The publishers' policy is to use paper manufactured from sustainable forests.

1 The Chicken that Came to Market

When Tom arrived at the market, Jamie and Zed had done no unpacking at all.

"What shall I do with this?" said Zed, by way of 'hello'.

This was a very large and glossy chicken. It had taken occupation of Zed's stall, and looked determined to stay. It stood firmly on the bare wood, braced on sturdy, scaly legs. It looked at Tom with one bright brown eye, then turned its head to look at him with the other.

"Eat it for lunch, with chips?" Jamie said. But Zed, who was vegetarian, pulled a face and shook his head.

"How'd it get here?" Tom asked.

"Good question," said Zed. "I've no idea. Jamie and I turned our backs for five minutes to start unloading, and there it was."

"Why did the chicken cross the market?" Jamie

said. "Because it wanted to get to the other side."

Tom couldn't help turning to look, to see what might interest a chicken on any of the market square's four sides. What he could see, through the aisles of stalls with their red-and-white striped awnings, was bits of shop fronts, a café with a blackboard propped outside on the pavement, and the fancy brickwork pattern on the front of the post office. Nothing of much interest to a chicken, as far as he could see.

"But it hasn't crossed the market," he pointed out. "It's stopped here. On Zed's stall."

"The point is, what shall I do with it?" Zed said. "It looks like it might give quite a hard peck if we try to catch it. And even if we do, then what? I need to move the van in the next ten minutes."

Tom looked along the row of stalls. "No one here sells live chickens! There's a butcher, but I don't think he does pick-your-own."

"Sell it, bruv!" Jamie suggested. "Free-range chicken, on the hoof!"

The chicken cocked its head and gave him a stern look.

"You've got plenty of boxes," Tom said to Zed. "Empty out that big one, and we'll see if we can get the chicken inside. Then you can put it in the van."

"But it must belong to someone," Zed pointed out. "I don't want to be arrested for hen-napping. Or chicken harassment. Or poultry hostage-taking."

"You can put a sign up on the stall – 'Found, one chicken'," Tom suggested. "Then its owner can claim it. But I don't see why anyone'd bring a huge great chicken to market in the first place."

The chicken was getting bored, scratching at the table where all Zed's goods ought to have been laid out by now.

"It's hungry," Jamie said.

"You know what – it's a pretty good specimen, isn't it?" Zed remarked. "I mean, when you think of most chickens these days, the ones that spend their lives cooped up in factory farms. All pink and helpless. This isn't the same sort of chicken at all. I mean, this is what you *call* a chicken."

Tom had to agree that it was a very fine chicken. With its strong legs, plumed tail and glossy feathers of russet and speckly brown, it was the sort of chicken he'd seen in picture books about farmyards, when he'd first started to read.

But the chicken was still at large, Zed's stall was due to open, and most of the stuff was still in the van. "Come on. We've got to do something about catching her," he said.

Jamie – always keen to leap into action – threw off his coat. "Get that box ready, bro'," he told Zed. "I'll bundle my coat over it and take it by surprise."

"Be careful," Zed warned. He emptied out the contents of a large box while the chicken watched with interest. Jamie, obviously imagining himself faced with some dangerous wild animal, flung his coat, made a grab, and shouted, "Gotcha!"

After a few moments of muffled squawking, the chicken fell silent.

"You haven't hurt her, have you?" Zed asked
anxiously.

"Nah." Jamie ushered the coat towards the
tipped-up box. "Knows when she's beaten, that's
all. Get ready to shut the lid."

"Now what?" said Zed, looking worried, when
the chicken was safely boxed. "If she's going to
wait in the van all day, she'll need something to
eat and drink. I'll have to go to the pet stall. What
d'you think she'd like?"

"We'll do the stall," Tom offered. "Get the
boxes out, then you can go and sort things out in
the van."

Zed was Jamie's older brother – 'my barmy
brother', Jamie called him. Zed ran the stall, but
was no businessman. Two years ago he'd started
on a business studies course, but had soon decided
that he didn't like any of the businesses
he'd come across. 'Small is Beautiful'
was his new motto. What he wanted to
do – what he did now – was make
things and sell them: bits of
jewellery, candlesticks, decorated
mirrors, little ornaments made of
twisted metal. He was his own
boss, with Tom and Jamie as
occasional helpers. He barely

9

scraped a living, but that was all he wanted. He went to Mapplesham Market on Saturdays and to Windlesham every other Wednesday; he lived in a rented caravan, did his metalwork, and was happy. Tom liked that about Zed. He owned practically nothing, but wanted no more.

Zed was for Zachary, but Zachary wasn't his real name either – he'd started life as Jack, then decided at eighteen that he'd rather choose his own name. Tom had no idea what had made him pick on Zachary – all he knew was that everyone, even Zed and Jamie's parents, now called Zed 'Zed'.

Jamie and Tom helped him every Saturday for pocket money – not much, as Zed couldn't afford it, but they both liked the market, and there wasn't much else to do in Mapplesham. Even on a raw, wintry day like today, there was always something or someone interesting. Zed's stall was a bit different from most. He sold things for friends, too, so the stall was never quite the same from one week to the next. There might be scented candles, beaded belts and wallets, small paintings, frames for photographs, plant pots. Now, with Christmas coming, he'd made lots of candlesticks and tiny tree decorations. Part of the fun, for Tom, was seeing what was in the van each week.

Today, while Zed drove round to the car park,
Tom and Jamie spread a blue and silver cloth over
the bare stall, and unpacked the boxes. There
were several dozen decorated candles, two stands
of earrings and necklaces, a boxful of belts with
buckles made to look like twisted snakes, a stack
of painted flowerpots, two boxes of tree
decorations, a thick folded wodge of Indian
shawls, and a jingly thing made of tubes.

Zed's stall was between Bill and Mary's fruit
and veg on one side, and baby clothes on the
other. Bill was arranging his boxes of potatoes,

tomatoes, onions and carrots on grassy green fabric.

His wife Mary, muffled up in a woolly hat and scarf, was spiking bunches of bananas to hang at the front of the stall.

"Bill," Tom called out, while he draped the Indian shawls, "you don't know anyone who's lost a chicken, do you? Zed's found one."

"Chicken?" Bill looked puzzled. "Hear that, Mary?"

Mary laughed. "You've found a chicken, have you? Well, this is what *we've* found."

She bent down behind the stall and lifted up a small basket lined with straw and containing six speckled, brown eggs.

The boys stared.

"You didn't see who left them?" Tom asked.

Bill shook his head. "No. I was getting the boxes out, and Mary was in the back of the van getting the Calor gas lit for a brew-up. When we looked at the stall again, there they were. Thought someone had left them for a present, but we don't know anyone who keeps hens."

"Well, someone left a great big hen on Zed's stall," Tom said. "He didn't see who, either."

"Whoever it is must get up early," Bill said. "There's no one much around, this time of day, only the stallholders."

"So which came first, the chicken or the eggs?" Mary wondered.

Jamie examined the speckled eggs, moving them aside and looking at the straw underneath. "Weird, isn't it? I mean, if there was someone lurking around, you'd expect them to be nicking stuff, not leaving things as presents. Specially not chickens and eggs."

Tom took the basket from Jamie and held it up. It was a proper little basket, handmade, carefully woven from wicker – the sort of basket Zed might sell on his stall. If whoever-it-was had only intended to give Bill and Mary some eggs, why didn't he or she put them in an ordinary cardboard egg-box?

He looked at Jamie. "There's something funny going on here."

"There is," Jamie agreed. "Something that needs investigating."

2 The Mapplesham Market Maze

"I've decided to call her Erica," Zed said when he came back from the car park. "Assuming she's a she."

"The chicken?" Tom asked. "Why Erica?"

"It was my grandmother's name," said Zed. "Mine and Jamie's. She seems quite happy – the chicken, I mean. I've bought her some grain, and a bowl for drinking-water, and some hay for nesting."

"So you're going to keep her, then?" Tom wasn't sure how wise it was for Zed to start calling the chicken Erica and getting fond of her – she might be claimed by the end of the day. He knew what Zed was like for adopting animals. Zed already shared his caravan with two cats and a kitten, an old collie with three legs, and a parakeet. There would hardly be room for Zed himself if he took in any more.

Tom fetched a piece of card and a felt-tip pen from the box under the stall, and wrote in capitals:

> FOUND, ONE LARGE HEN. ANY INFORMATION ABOUT IT'S OWNER WILL BE GRATEFULLY RECIEVED.

"You mean *its*, no apostrophe," Zed pointed out. "And you spell *received* with an *e-i*, not an *i-e*."

"Oh, all right," Tom said. He hadn't known Zed was so strict about spelling and punctuation. He wrote it all again on the other side of the card, then pinned the sign to the front of the stall. "We've got everything ready. Shall we fetch your breakfast?"

Zed was always in too much of a hurry to eat breakfast first thing, and as he hardly ever remembered to go shopping for food, Tom viewed it as his and Jamie's responsibility to make sure he was properly fed. Breakfast was usually a mug of tea and a peanut butter sandwich from the van at the corner of the market.

"Thanks!" Zed sorted coins from his bum-bag and handed them over. "Get yourselves something, too. Warm yourselves up."

Zed was the one who needed warming up. For some reason he never wore enough clothes. Today, it was cold enough for all the other stallholders to be well wrapped up in coats, scarves and fingerless gloves, but Zed wore a thin holey jumper with a T-shirt underneath, and had to keep banging his arms against his sides to keep warm.

Frank, at the burger van, wasn't in a good mood. "Don't know how I'm going to make ends meet, with that new place just opened up!" he was complaining to Dot from the plant stall, handing her a bacon sandwich. He glared at the new fast-food restaurant, Quiksnax, that had just opened on the corner of the square. "One of those big chains, that is – you get 'em at motorway services, so why bother with an out-of-the-way little place like Mapplesham? Takeaways an' all, they do."

Tom and Jamie didn't stay to talk, as Frank didn't seem in the mood. They bought Zed's tea and sandwich, and hot chocolate for themselves, then went back to see if the stall had any customers.

There was just one – Sadia, whose parents ran the fashion stall two aisles down. She was looking at the carved wooden earrings and talking to Zed. Jamie nudged Tom and grinned. Sadia was a regular visitor. She had glossy hair and dark brown eyes and a soft voice that rippled easily into laughter. She laughed a lot when she was talking to Zed. Zed gazed back at her, all gooey.

Jamie made a soppy face. "He won't want us around now. How about we check out the whole market – see if anyone else has got chickens or eggs?"

Tom nodded, and handed Zed his breakfast. "Back in a little while, okay?" he told him. Zed nodded, hardly noticing.

"The Maze, right?" Jamie said to Tom, in a low voice, as they walked away.

The Mapplesham Market Maze was Jamie's invention. Only he and Tom knew about it. It was a way of using the gaps between stalls, the aisles, the edges of the market square and the alleyways between shops and buildings, to pass every shop and stall. Jamie's rules were strict – you must never cross your own tracks, and you must never walk down the whole stretch twice.

It was quite complicated and had taken a lot of working out. Jamie kept the route stored in his head, but Tom, who liked to be methodical, had drawn a diagram at home, on which he'd marked every single stall and every gap, and drawn the maze route in green, with arrows to show the direction of travel. He and Jamie refreshed their memories by doing the whole route at least once a fortnight. The trick was to do it all in one go, without getting lost, without having to stop to work out where to go next, and without getting told off by stallholders when you darted through the gaps where shoppers didn't usually go. Most importantly, you must never let anyone know what you were doing. It was Jamie and Tom's secret. They knew every corner, every dustbin, every pile of boxes. If anyone was doing any funny business with chickens and eggs, Tom and Jamie stood a good chance of finding out.

"Start at the usual place?" Jamie said.

Tom nodded. "It's confusing if you start anywhere else."

They dodged through the gap between Zed's stall and Bill and Mary's, and went to the old market cross in front of the post office. The cross, made of worn, lichen-encrusted stone, was the finishing post as well as the start. From here, you left the market square immediately, going down a narrow alleyway between the post office and the public toilets. Then you had to go round the back of the toilets, along Piper's Alley, and back to the square between a sweet shop and a bank. Next, you went along almost the whole of one side, passing a small row of very smart shops – selling jewellery, expensive chocolates, wines and books respectively – and then a right-hand bend past a florist's, a small computer shop called Bitz and Bytes, to the new fast-food restaurant, before entering the avenues of market stalls for the first time. But Tom and Jamie didn't get as far as the stalls, because there, on the thin strip of road that bordered the square, a police car was parked. Inside the computer shop stood two tall policemen.

"We'd better stop here for a minute." Jamie always took charge when they were navigating the Maze. "It's not really breaking the rule about not stopping, because we're on a special mission today."

19

"You think the computer shop's had a visit, too?" Tom said.

"Well, *some*thing's happened. It may be connected."

A poultry invasion, perhaps? Tom couldn't hear any squawks or cackles, but he could see the shop manager talking to the policemen in great agitation – waving his arms about, a bit like a flustered chicken himself. A small group of people gathered on the pavement.

"Burglars," said a man who had been there the longest. "Manager says he never heard the alarm go off, though."

One of the policemen came to the door and looked out at the market, turning his head from side to side to see who was around. Tom hoped he and Jamie wouldn't be taken for suspects. Two boys, hanging around doing nothing very much – some of the stallholders had been suspicious of them at first, thinking they were up to no good, until they'd got used to them, and realised they were Zed's helpers.

A few moments later, the second policeman came out, putting away a notebook, and they both got in their car and drove away.

"Let's go in," Jamie said, "and find out what's been nicked."

"That'll look a bit nosey, won't it?" Tom pointed out.

"I don't care. I want to know what's happened. 'Sides, my dad needs a new mouse for his PC. I can ask how much they are."

"Okay, then." Tom wasn't sure – the manager seemed to be just as grumpy as Frank at the burger van had been. But he followed Jamie in, and they didn't have to ask any questions, because another man was asking, "Trouble, then, Gordon?"

"You can say that again," the manager said, a bit red-faced. "Someone's nicked a laptop!" He was lifting a new one into the gap on the shelf. "Some joker, if you ask me. Somehow, he manages to get in and out without setting the alarm off. And he leaves me a turkey."

Tom caught his breath, and exchanged glances with Jamie, while the other man repeated, "A turkey?"

"What, a live one?" Tom couldn't help asking.

The manager, Gordon, gave him a cross look. "Of course not a live one." He bent down behind his counter and held up a large plucked turkey by its legs. It was so big that he had to strain to lift it, getting even redder in the face. The feathers had been left on its head and neck, so it didn't look like the ones you got in the supermarket, all plucked and pink and ready for the oven – it looked like a real, dead, turkey.

"Found it on the shelf where the computer was," Gordon said. "The police thought I was making it up, till I showed them."

"It's quite a nice one," the other man said, admiring the corpse. "Do you for Christmas, that will, if you put it in the freezer."

Tom noticed a few bronze-coloured feathers on the carpet. Most turkeys he'd seen had white feathers, or sometimes black.

"Huh!" Gordon said, grumpily. "Rather have the laptop back. What do you two want, anyway?" he added, glaring at Tom and Jamie. "Come to enjoy the fun, have you?"

Tom pulled a face at Jamie and they made a quick exit. *Not* a good time to ask about the mouse.

3 Hooked Fish

"It looks to me," Tom said, outside Bitz and Bytes, "as if the thief's paying for things with chickens and eggs and turkeys. You know, bartering? Like people do sometimes, in places where there's no money or they don't want to bother with it. Two lettuces in exchange for a jug of milk; that sort of thing."

"But nothing was taken from Zed, or Bill," Jamie pointed out.

"Perhaps it was," Tom said. "Zed might not have noticed. He's not very good at noticing things. And Bill and Mary have got loads of stuff, haven't they, in different boxes? It'd be easy enough for the thief to take a bunch of carrots or something."

"But," Jamie objected, "if he's paying with eggs and hens, he's not really a thief, is he?"

"Or she," Tom said. "It might be a she. Well, I don't know."

He considered the problem. "I mean, to do that bartering business, both people have to agree to it, don't they? That's the whole point of it. You can't just help yourself to things and leave a bunch of radishes, or whatever you've got, for the other person to like it or lump it. And I don't know how much a laptop costs, but I wouldn't have thought a turkey was a fair exchange. Even a big turkey, like that."

"I'm getting cold," Jamie said. "Come on, let's get on with the Maze. We might find out something else." He giggled suddenly.

"What's up?" Tom asked.

"I was just thinking, what if we all started using chickens instead of money? 'Here's your pocket money, Jamie – two chicken legs.'"

Tom grinned. "Yes, and 'Can you change a ten-pound turkey? I haven't got anything smaller.'"

"And beggars would put egg-boxes on the pavement in front of them instead of hats," Jamie said, "and they'd say, 'Spare me a free-range brown, mister?'"

Thinking of sillier and sillier examples, they took the Maze's first turn into the avenues of stalls. This meant crossing the narrow road, passing to the right of a raised flower bed planted with winter pansies. Then back into the market proper, going between Sadia's family's fashion stall, hung with dresses, skirts and sweaters, and a stall that sold toys and games. The owner of the toy stall wasn't very friendly towards Tom and Jamie, mainly because of their habit of appearing unexpectedly from between the stalls. Their private name for him was Mr Miserable. At the moment he was scowling over his display of pink teddies, plastic elephants and board games.

"Hi there, Tom, Jamie," came a voice from behind the dangling scarves on the other side. It was Mr Safadi, Sadia's father. Sadia wasn't there – still talking to Zed, Tom guessed. Mr Safadi emerged, smiling and cheerful as usual – not looking anxious or baffled. There was no sign that he'd come into unexpected contact with poultry, alive or dead.

Tom and Jamie stopped to pursue their enquiries.

"You haven't had anything taken this morning, have you?" Tom asked.

"No. We saw the police car, but we haven't seen anything," Mr Safadi said. "We keep our eyes open."

It was most odd, Tom thought. Everyone kept their eyes open – market stallholders had to be good at that – yet someone was strolling about with chickens and turkeys, unseen and unnoticed.

"I wonder what the thief did with the laptop?" he asked Jamie, as they walked on. "It's not the sort of thing you could slip into your pocket."

"Must have had a getaway car parked handy," Jamie suggested. "Behind the computer shop."

"So he'll have cleared off half an hour ago," Tom said. "All the same, it's worth a look round."

The Maze now took them past the toy stall to one that sold all sorts of old-fashioned sweets – toffees, bulls' eyes, coconut ice, different kinds of fudge – displayed in big jars. The boys often stopped here, and Jamie delved into his pocket for change.

"Forty pence worth of mint humbugs, please," he asked Marion, who kept the stall. She weighed them out on her scales and tipped them into a paper bag.

"Have you seen anyone strange this morning?" Tom asked.

Marion smiled. "Depends what you mean by 'strange'. There's those two over there, for a start." She nodded towards the hot dog van, where two bikers stood, dressed in black studded leather. They clutched their helmets as they drank coffee from polystyrene cups. They both had long, straggly, grey hair and were much older than Tom's and Jamie's dads.

"Doug and Derek?" Jamie said. "They're not strange. They're here most weeks."

"It's strange to my way of thinking," Marion said. "Dressing like Hell's Angels when they're old enough to be grandads, the pair of them."

"Hell's Grandads?" said Jamie.

"So you haven't had anything stolen today?" Tom asked. "Or anything left here?"

Marion shook her head. "One customer left her purse and I had to run after her with it, but no,

28

nothing taken. I'm sure I'd have noticed."

The boys walked on, sucking Jamie's humbugs. The Maze path, at this point, had to do a small detour to fit in the cheese van, which insisted on parking at an angle instead of keeping to straight lines like everyone else. It obviously wanted to emphasise its status as van, not stall. Next, the route passed through one of its most perilous sections: a central strip, barred to the public, where the stalls were back-to-back, leaving a long narrow alleyway, or roofless tunnel, that ran the whole width of the market. Here, the stall owners stored their boxes, empty or full, and various other clutter. Not realising that anyone used the tunnel as a thoroughfare, they often stacked boxes haphazardly across the route, so that it was like an obstacle course. The challenge was to get all the way through in one go, without being stopped or told off. Stallholders were apt to be suspicious of anyone they found lurking in restricted areas.

But today, Tom knew it was vital to check out the central tunnel. If someone was hiding chickens, turkeys or computers in the market, this would be the best place to do it. Someone might be sneaking things in behind the stalls while no one was looking.

Tom took a deep breath at the entrance. To get in, you had to lift a flap of awning – then you saw the shadowy tunnel, striped red and white, stretching ahead of you.

"Ready?" Jamie whispered.

"Yeah!" Tom whispered back.

And they were off, between screens of plastic
that were pegged aside for access, giving glimpses
of various stallholders' back views as the boys
passed. They dashed behind the flower stall,
avoiding buckets full of dahlias and carnations.
Darted along the back of the shoe stall,
clambering over boxes stacked higgledy-piggledy
with tartan slippers falling out. Scrambled over
secondhand books, packed tightly in boxes,
smelling of must and mildew. Usually, the aim was
to get to the other end as quickly as possible, but
today – keeping close to Jamie's heels – Tom took

care to look round for anything strange or out of place. As he passed between pet foods on his left and knitting wool on his right, one of the customers at the pet stall looked straight at him, drawing the attention of the stallholder, who turned and made a grab.

"Oi! You! Gotcha!"

Tom was snatched by the hood of his fleece, and powerful arms dragged him out of the tented alleyway and into public view. He was swivelled round, and an angry face appeared in front of him: a man's face, red, angry, beneath a cloth cap. Tom felt like a fish hoiked out of the water for everyone to gaze at. A small crowd gathered, staring. Jamie, the faster runner of the two, was nowhere to be seen.

"Boys!" sneered a headscarfed woman. She was the customer who'd first spotted Tom. "You've got to have eyes in the back of your head."

Pet Shop Man glowered at Tom. Still held by his hood, Tom noticed how much the man resembled a bulldog. He'd always felt that bulldogs were unpredictable, with their grumpy faces – you never knew when they might snarl or snap at

you. Pet Shop Man looked as if he'd like to give
Tom a good hard bite. He was almost growling.

"I heard there was thieving going on," he snarled.
"So it's you, is it, sneaking round the back to get
your thieving little hands on my stuff – you and that
whippersnapper friend of yours? You won't do that
again if you know what's good for you!"

Tom tried to step back and got tangled up in a
hanging forest of dog leads. Then he stumbled
over a pile of plastic feeding bowls, scattering
them at Pet Shop Man's feet.

Pet Shop Man tutted, as if Tom had done it on

purpose. "Mind where you're putting your clodhopping feet!"

"I haven't stolen anything," Tom protested. "Honest I haven't!"

"They all say that," said Headscarf Woman, propping herself against the side of the stall to enjoy the argument. "There was a police car here a few minutes ago," she told Pet Shop Man. "I'd hand him straight over if I were you."

"I've got my mobile," said someone else. "Shall I dial 999?"

"No, wait!" Tom pleaded. "Look, I haven't taken anything, I promise! I'll turn my pockets out if you like."

Pet Shop Man let go of Tom's hood, but he said, "Oh yeah? And what have you done with that bag of chicken pellets you took?"

"*What* bag of chicken pellets? I've only just got here!"

"Oh yes, and we saw *how* you got here." Pet
Shop Man jutted his chin at
Tom. "Down the back
of the stall. Does that
look like an honest
paying customer?"
he appealed to his
audience.

"But I'm not a customer. I wasn't going to buy anything," Tom said.

"Exactly." The chin jutted another three centimetres in Tom's direction. "Not going to buy anything. That's just what I'm complaining about. Nicking it instead. Otherwise, why lurk round the back?"

"I was just taking a short cut," Tom mumbled. He couldn't mention the Maze! Not even Zed knew about the Mapplesham Market Maze, even though the boys had to go right past his stall when they were following it.

"Oh yeah? In a hurry, were you?" Pet Shop Man said.

"What's the problem, Tom?" called a friendly voice, and Tom turned to see Sadia peering over the shoulders of the accusing crowd.

"Nicked a bag of chicken pellets, he has," Pet Shop Man told her. "And hasn't even got the bottle to own up."

"No, 'cos I didn't take it!" Tom insisted.

"Course you did. Nicked it for that hippy mate of yours – him with the candles and tie-dye! He's got a chicken, hasn't he? Bought some stuff only this morning. Send you back for more, did he?"

"No! He wouldn't!" Tom was outraged. Someone had stolen chicken pellets, but Zed was the last person in the world who would ever think of stealing. "Okay, he's got a chicken now, but he paid for his stuff, didn't he? There's someone else ..."

Pet Shop Man wasn't listening to Tom. He went on, "Waited till my back was turned for two minutes, this young hoodlum did, and ..."

"I can assure you," Sadia said firmly, "that whatever's been stolen, Tom wasn't responsible. And neither was Zed. Come on, Tom. Let's go back to Zed's stall." And she stepped forward, parting the crowd, and took Tom by the arm. "I should be very careful about making accusations in future," she told Pet Shop Man. "You could end up in a lot of trouble."

"Lot of fuss about nothing, if you ask me," someone said, and the crowd began to disperse.

As Tom followed Sadia past Pet Shop Man's sacks of dog biscuits and wild birdseed, he noticed something tucked in neatly between the bags – a small wicker basket, containing six speckled eggs and one rust-coloured feather.

4 Barter System

"Thanks a lot, Jamie," Tom humphed, back at the stall. Zed was rearranging his display of belts, and Jamie was sitting on a pile of boxes at the back, still sucking humbugs. Sadia had gone back to her own stall.

With both cheeks full, Jamie made a comment that sounded like 'Whawr?'

"It was really nice of you to clear off and leave me in enemy clutches," Tom went on. "I'll do the same for you some day."

"What use would it have been if we'd both got caught?" Jamie argued. "At least one of us was free to come back to base and carry out further investigations."

"I really enjoyed being yanked out and displayed to everyone like 'Specimen A'," Tom went on. "Having everyone stare at me like I was a criminal. Anyway, *what* further investigations?

You're just sitting there stuffing yourself, as far as I can see."

Jamie tapped the side of his head. "It's brainwork that counts. I've made an important discovery. Well, Zed has."

"What?"

"Zed's had his calculator nicked," Jamie said.

Zed ducked underneath a festoon of rainbow-coloured scarves, straightened up into a faceful of wind chimes and set them tinkling and jingling. "Yes," he said, looking worried. "Thing is, I don't know when. I looked for it just now to give to Jamie, and it was gone. I don't usually use it myself, not on the stall. Only when I do the accounts, Sundays."

"No, well – some of us can do simple mental arithmetic," Tom said, to get back at Jamie, "and some of us can't. So who's been looking at the stall? Anyone peculiar? Anyone furtive?"

"No," Jamie said. "All I've sold is three pairs of earrings, a scarf and a candle. All to one person – that's why I wanted the calculator."

"I haven't sold anything at all," said Zed, "because till Jamie came back I was, er, talking to Sadia –"

"Chatting her up, he means," Jamie interrupted.

" – talking to Sadia," Zed repeated, blushing, "and no one else was here. The calculator must have gone before Jamie sold the earrings and things, because that's when I realised it was missing."

"Hmm." Tom considered the new development. "So when's the last time you can actually remember seeing it?"

Zed frowned. "I think it must have been quite early, when I was setting stuff out. I remember putting it on the bare table. I can't remember seeing it again."

"Before the chicken?" Tom asked. "You mean the calculator could have gone at the same time as the chicken arrived?"

"I suppose so," said Zed. "But perhaps I'd better have another look through these spare boxes. Maybe I dropped it in without noticing."

He crouched behind the trestles and started

burrowing through a box of T-shirts. Jamie looked at Tom. "Your idea about paying for things is beginning to make sense," he said. "A turkey for a computer. A chicken for a calculator."

"A basket of eggs for chicken feed," Tom said, then, remembering that Jamie didn't know about the theft from the pet stall, he explained about that one.

"But what about Bill and Mary?" Jamie said, nodding his head towards the next-door stall. "They got a basket of eggs for nothing, didn't they? They didn't have anything nicked."

"Let's ask," Tom said. "They might have discovered something."

Tom didn't know how Bill could keep shouting all day the way he did, in his foghorn voice that carried right across the market. Perhaps that was why Mary wore her woolly hat pulled right down, so that she wasn't deafened by the constant ear blasting. They were both busy, dealing with a queue of customers.

"GRAPEFRUITS FOUR FOR A PAHND," Bill was bellowing, tipping Brussels sprouts into a paper bag, then twirling the bag shut with a deft flick of his wrists. "COME AND GET YOUR LOVELY GRAPEFRUITS. BEST MUSHROOMS ON THE MARKET. BAG OF JUICY SATSUMAS, ONLY NINETY PENCE TODAY. HERE YOU ARE, LOVE – TWENTY-THREE PENCE CHANGE. COME AND GET YOUR –"

Not liking to interrupt, Tom had to join the queue. He reached Mary first.

"Yes, love? Found any other strange goings-on?" she asked.

Tom told her about the various thefts, then said, "You know that basket of eggs that was left here, first thing? You didn't notice anything missing, did you, afterwards?"

"Well, you know, it's funny you should ask," Mary said. "Because when I came to serve a customer with kiwi fruit, I noticed someone'd already been in the box. It was full right up when we packed it in the van." She showed Tom the box – the green tray with indentations about the size and shape of eggs, some empty now. "And I hadn't sold any this morning till then. I reckon someone had helped themselves to one."

"Hmm. Kiwi fruit," Tom said thoughtfully. "And left the eggs in payment."

"SPECIAL OFFER ON CAULIFLAHS, ONLY 45p EACH," Bill hollered into his left ear. "CHESTNUTS, LOVELY FOR ROASTING –"

"Not such a good exchange then, really!" Mary said. "I'd have given him *two* kiwi fruits for six eggs, if he'd asked," and she turned to her next customer.

Tom went back to tell Zed and Jamie what he'd found out. "The next step," he decided, "is to make a list of all the things that have gone missing. There must be some pattern. Some reason behind it."

"Chicken feed and calculators? Computers and kiwi fruit?" said Zed, frowning. "If there's a pattern there, I can't see it."

"Got a notebook and pencil?" Tom asked.

Zed handed them over, and Tom divided a page into three columns. Then he wrote:

Things stolen or taken	Where from	Things left
1 calculator	Zed's	1 large chicken (Erica)
1 kiwi fruit	Bill and Mary's	6 eggs in basket
1 laptop	Bitz + Bytes	1 large turkey (dead)
1 bag chicken pellets	Pet food stall	6 eggs in basket

He showed the list to Zed and Jamie. "So where does that leave us?"

"Computer-whizz chicken fancier?" Zed said doubtfully.

"Pickpocket poultry farmer?" Tom suggested.

"Chicken promoter?" said Zed. "Market vandal?"

"There must be some pattern," Tom insisted. He looked at Jamie. "Do you think we ought to – you know – carry on where we left off?"

"What, get caught by Pet Shop Man again?" Jamie said.

Tom didn't fancy that! "What we'll do," he told Jamie, "is start again. Ask at every single stall whether anything's been nicked today, or left behind. Get a complete list. Then, if there's a pattern, we're more likely to see it."

But they drew a blank. Nothing else had been taken that day, and nothing strange left behind. Not a single egg or stray feather.

5 J.S.

Tom and Jamie had to wait until the following
Saturday for another chance to solve the Market
Mystery. They had agreed to meet at Jamie's
house a little earlier than usual, wanting to be at
the market in time to help Zed set out the stall. It
was a cold, drizzly morning, the sort of morning
when it would have been far nicer to stay in bed.
But the Mystery awaited, and Tom was
determined to be present when the next curious
exchange took place. He hoped there would be
more. It occurred to him, as he laced his trainers,
that it would be a bit dull if nothing out of the
ordinary happened at all today – if people only
bought things with money, instead of secretively
exchanging them for eggs or poultry. What if the
poultry barterer had visited for one day only?

"You know what?" he said, as he and Jamie
hurried along the dismal streets, heads down.

"What?" Jamie was yawning, half asleep.

"Well. I've been wondering if the thief – barterer – whatever he is, or she is, might be a – well, a – you know, a –"

"A what?"

"A ghost," Tom said.

There, he'd said it now. Jamie's mouth snapped shut in mid yawn and he gave Tom a sceptical look.

"A ghost? You kidding?"

"Well, the town hall's supposed to be haunted, so why shouldn't the market be?"

"You don't believe in all that rubbish, do you? My mum says it's just someone's bright idea to bring tourists in. I mean, she works in the town hall, and she's never seen it!"

"Not sure," said Tom. The town hall ghost was supposedly a white-faced young woman who stalked the upper floors and gazed sorrowfully out of the windows on moonless nights. "But maybe there's a market ghost. How else could someone raid three different stalls and a shop without anyone noticing? I mean, *once* you might believe, but *four times*?"

"You're off your trolley," Jamie said, opening a packet of chewing gum. "That chicken – Erica – wasn't a ghost chicken, was she? Larger than life if you ask me. If she'd given you a peck with that great sharp beak, it wouldn't have been a ghostly peck, I can tell you." He laughed, mockingly. "Ghost! Wait till I tell Zed!"

"No, don't," Tom said hastily. Now that Jamie had scoffed at the idea, it sounded as ridiculous as it probably was.

The striped awnings were shiny with rain, and the market full of early morning bustle as the stallholders got ready. Zed had put out most of his things, and had already moved the van round to the car park. He was shivering in his holey jumper – didn't he own a coat? Tom wondered – but had put on a black knitted hat and a yellow Rupert Bear scarf. He showed Tom and Jamie the last few boxes that needed unpacking.

"How's Erica?" Tom asked, unpacking a box of twisted metal candlesticks.

"Fine, thanks. I've made a big run for her." Zed was hanging up a selection of batik T-shirts so that the colours showed themselves off: he put yellow against purple, orange against turquoise, green against maroon. "But I think she's a bit lonely. I'm wondering whether to get another couple of chickens, for company."

"I'd wait, if I were you," Tom advised. "You never know what might turn up today. Was it Windlesham Wednesday? Anything funny happen there?"

"No, nothing," Zed said. "Except Pet Shop Man giving me a funny look when I went to buy chicken pellets. I'm on the stall next to him at Windlesham, and I know he doesn't like me. I'm sure he thinks I'm something to do with the strange goings-on. Now I'm a chicken-keeper, I'm number one suspect. Did quite well this week, though." He took a five-pound note out of his bum-bag. "So well, that I'm going to treat myself to a new calculator. Do you want to go and get one for me? You know Brian – secondhand

books and stationery? See if he's got one."

The market was open for business by now and the first shoppers were arriving, huddled beneath umbrellas, comparing prices. The smell of hot dogs and onions floated across the square. Tom and Jamie splashed through puddles to Brian's stall. It was in two halves: one side loaded with secondhand books, the other with pens, pencils, rubbers and notebooks. Tom and Jamie chose a calculator, then lingered – Jamie wanted a new pencil case and couldn't choose between Man United and Chelsea, as he claimed to support both, and Tom got engrossed in a book about black holes. Brian, a big man in a green waxed coat and a brown waxed hat, went back to tidying up stray books.

"Hey, you two!" he exclaimed suddenly. "You

were asking last week about any strange customers, weren't you? Looks like someone's left me a message."

He held out a scrap of paper. It was cream-coloured with torn edges, and written on it in ink was:

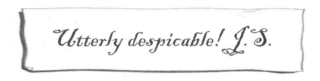

Utterly despicable! J.S.

Tom turned the paper over and rubbed it between his fingers.

It was thick but smooth, and the handwriting was done in proper fountain pen, the ink thick and black. Tom could see where the nib had splayed out at the bottom of the 'y'. But no, not fountain pen. He looked more closely and could see the ink fading by the end of 'despicable', then darker again where the writer had dipped it in ink for 'J.S.'

"That's calligraphy, that is," Jamie said. "My auntie can do that."

"Where d'you find it?" Tom asked Brian.

"Sticking out of this book here." Brian picked up a thick paperback and held it up briefly for the boys to see. *Midsummer Nights*, Tom saw, and a man and a woman embracing against a sunset background.

Jamie sniggered.

"It looks a bit racy," Brian said, "though I haven't read it myself, of course. Obviously J.S. doesn't like it, whoever he is. Must have taken it last week, and brought it back today when I wasn't looking. Daft, really, just putting it back with the others like that. I'd have swapped it for another if he'd asked."

"J.S.," Tom said thoughtfully. He felt sure this must be the best clue yet to the identity of the mystery marketeer. "Whose initials are J.S.? And how did he get the book in the first place?" he asked Brian. "Did he pay for it?"

Brian pursed up his mouth, thinking hard for a moment. "Can't say I remember. He could have swapped it." He pointed to a sign at the side of his stall. "I do a book swap, see, as well as  selling them. You bring me one book – long as it's in reasonable nick – and you take another."

"Oh yes?" Tom said eagerly. "Did you get a book in exchange for this one, then?"

Brian thought again. "It's funny," he said, "but

I can't remember anyone buying it or doing a swap. My mind's a blank."

Tom was struck by a thought. "He might have just put his own book on the rack, without telling you. He's like that."

"How do you know what he's like?" Brian said, giving him an odd look.

"Oh, just an idea," Tom said quickly. "Can we go through them all? In case there's anything here you haven't seen before?"

"What's the point?" Jamie said. "How are we going to know? And anyway, one tatty old book in exchange for another – what's that going to tell us?"

"Here, watch it," Brian said sharply. "My books aren't tatty. I only take books in a good state of repair, like I said. Yes, all right," he told Tom. "But I don't suppose you'll find anything."

"Tell you what," Jamie said, bored with standing still. "I'll go round all the other stalls and see if anyone else has got a calligraphy message."

"Good idea. But if they have," Tom said, "make sure you make a note of where the message was, like in this *Midsummer Nights* book. That's important."

Jamie set off, and Tom started at one end of a

row of books displayed spine-up. They were nearly all paperbacks: thrillers, romances, horror stories, a few Westerns. Nothing very exciting, and certainly nothing that matched his idea of J.S. He was beginning to feel disappointed, when Brian lifted another box of books from under the counter, plucked something out and gave a yelp of surprise. "Well, knock me sideways! Look at this!"

6 Kiwi Fruit

Brian was holding up a book – a small book, with a cover of dark green leather embellished in gold. He turned it over in his hands, then looked inside the cover and leafed through the pages.

"Wow, this must be worth a bit! *A Christmas Carol* by Charles Dickens! In perfect condition, too! I don't remember anyone swapping me this."

"*A Christmas Carol?*" Tom repeated. He'd seen the film on TV last Christmas. "The story about Scrooge?"

"That's the one. Look at this leather cover! Look at this gold lettering! Look at this paper! You don't see many books like this any more." Brian laughed. "'Specially not on my stall."

"So you've never seen it before?" Tom asked. "You've no idea how it got here?"

Brian shook his head. "Whoever brought it here must have been mad. You'd get a good price

for this if you took it to one of
them book fairs."

"Anything written in it?"
Tom asked, wondering
whether there was any
proof to link the book
with J.S. "Someone's
name?"

Brian looked
inside. "No. Nothing
written at all. But it's
got some dates. 'First
published 1843', it says.
'This edition 1890'."

"You're kidding! So that
book's more than a hundred years old?" Tom held
out his hand. "Can I see?"

"Here." Brian leaned forward so that water
dripped on his waxed hat from the front of the
awning. A drop fell on the book and he wiped it
off quickly. "Careful, mind. Reckon I'll get a good
price for that."

"Don't you want to keep it?" Tom said, turning
the pages and looking at the line illustrations. The
green leather was smooth in his hands. Who had
first bought this book? he wondered. Who had
first read it? And when?

Brian laughed. "Not if I can get a good price for it, no. Bit of a windfall, that is. I'd say, when J.S. swapped that for *Midsummer Nights*, he made a bad bargain."

"I wonder if J.S. wanted it back?" Tom suggested. "When he brought back the one he'd taken? If so, he couldn't have found it, could he – 'cos you had it in a box under the counter? That means he must have done the swap last week."

"He's not getting this back," Brian said, grinning. "No way. Call me Scrooge if you like, but this is mine now. He can have as many *Midsummer Nights* as he wants, but not this. If you see any old codger wandering about with books under his arm, point him my way." He took *A Christmas Carol* from Tom, wrapped it in a bag and stowed it carefully behind his stall.

Tom walked back to Zed's, thinking carefully. He'd come across three important clues, he decided: the initials J.S., *A Christmas Carol*, and the date, 1890.

"*A Christmas Carol's* a ghost story, isn't it?" he asked Zed.

"Yes, that's right." Zed was serving a group of giggling girls who kept changing their minds about various rings and necklaces. He didn't seem at all surprised to be asked such a question out of the blue.

"Hmm." Tom went round behind the stall. There was no sign of Jamie. "How long's this market been here?"

"Since about half-past seven this morning." Zed counted out change for one of the girls. "Usual sort of time."

"No, I mean in years," Tom explained.

"Oh, right. Well, it was here in medieval times, wasn't it? That market cross is dated fifteen hundred and something. And some of these buildings – the oldest ones, like the town hall – go back that far."

"And there's been a market here ever since?" Tom asked. "For more than four hundred years?"

"Far as I know," said Zed. "Why d'you ask?"

The girls wandered off, showing each other what they'd bought. Tom hesitated, unwilling to tell Zed about his ghost idea. Instead, he started telling him about the new clues, and was interrupted by Jamie rushing up and skidding to a halt, highly excited.

"Five more messages! I've got them all, look!"

He handed Tom a torn piece of cream paper. Tom read it and passed it to Zed.

"Look, it's signed J.S. as before!"

> *Wholly incomprehensible. J. S.*

"That one was in the computer shop," Jamie said. "And there's this one, found by Sadia's dad."

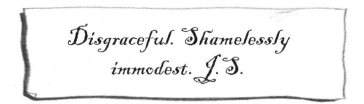

> *Disgraceful. Shamelessly immodest. J. S.*

"*What's* shamelessly immodest?" Tom said. "Where exactly was it left?"

"Pinned to some stuff hanging up at the front of the stall. Stretchy exercise gear – you know, crop-tops, leggings, that sort of thing," Jamie said. "And then this one."

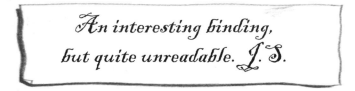

> *An interesting binding, but quite unreadable. J. S.*

Zed read aloud. "Where was this?"

"On the video stall," Jamie said. "And it was tucked in a video of *Martin Chuzzlewit*."

"*Martin Chuzzlewit*? That's Charles Dickens again!" said Zed. "J.S. must be a Dickens fan. But it looks as if he thought the video was a book, and was disappointed when he couldn't read it."

"Some kind of loony," Jamie said. "Must be, not to know what a video is! And here are the last two. Both from Quiksnax, you know, that new fast-food place on the corner. He obviously got hungry, but he didn't like their food. This one was on a paper plate, with a Quikchik burger – that's what they call them, no kidding – with only one mouthful out of it! I got the message just in time before the waitress chucked it in the bin."

> *Tasteless. Most unwholesome fare.*
> *A disgrace to the market and the*
> *goodfolk of Mapplesham. J. S.*

"Not an easy person to please, is he?" said Zed.

"And the other one?" Tom prompted.

"Aha," Jamie smirked. "Took a bit of initiative to get this. Asked the waitress if she'd seen any others – she said no, but then when she went back behind the counter, there was this, tucked under the corner of the till!" He handed it over with a flourish.

*The return of Quick,
or rather of Quiksnax as you
would have it? Effrontery!
Now that you have thrown
down a gauntlet, be sure that
I shall pick it up. J.S.*

Zed frowned at it. "What on earth?"

"'Thrown down a gauntlet'?" Tom read aloud.

"It means challenging someone," Zed explained. "Like picking a fight. One person throws a – well, a sort of glove, and that's making the challenge. If the other person picks it up, they've accepted. And 'effrontery' means cheek."

"So there's going to be a fight?" Jamie looked eagerly around the market as if he feared missing something.

"Well – not necessarily an actual fight, with punching and kicking," said Zed. "But I haven't a clue what all this 'return of Quick' stuff means."

"So all these messages have appeared this morning?" Tom asked Jamie.

"J.S. obviously did more shopping than we knew about," said Zed.

Jamie nodded. "I've checked everywhere. That's it for now. Who do you think J.S. is – some sort of market inspector?"

"Market inspectors wouldn't leave messages on torn-off bits of paper, would they?" Tom objected. "They'd type an official report, or something – not go on about gloves and gauntlets!"

"And this writing," Zed laid out all five messages in front of him on the stall. "I can't see why a market inspector would use such an old-fashioned pen. Look, you can see each time the nib's been dipped in the ink."

"Besides," Tom said, "he doesn't seem to know what things are for, does he? He says the computer is totally incomprehensible. He thinks a video's a book."

"And he likes using old-fashioned words," said Zed, "like 'unwholesome fare' and 'shamelessly immodest', and 'goodfolk', and 'effrontery'."

Tom looked at Jamie and then at Zed, wondering whether to mention the word 'ghost' again. He couldn't help seeing J.S. as someone from a different time – someone who found the market a mystifying place, full of inexplicable objects, skimpy clothing and unfamiliar foods.

"Kiwi fruit!" he exclaimed.

Both Zed and Jamie stared at him.

"What about them?" Jamie asked.

"There wouldn't have been kiwi fruit when he was around, would there?" Tom explained. "They don't come from this country, do they? And they haven't been around all that long – my Mum said she can remember having her first one, when she was about my age. J.S. had never seen them before, so he took some to try!"

Jamie was staring at him as if he'd gone barmy. "What d'you mean, when he was around?" he said. "He's around now, isn't he?"

"No, I don't mean that." Tom felt himself going red. "I meant, a hundred years ago. There were no kiwi fruits then. No hot dogs, either," he added.

"Don't be daft," Jamie scoffed. "Have you heard this lunatic idea of his?" he appealed to Zed. "He's got it into his head that there's a ghost wandering round the market – a ghost lugging round armfuls of chicken pellets and dead turkeys, and tucking into Quiksnax burgers and kiwi fruit. Funny kind of ghost – can you imagine it?" He waggled a thumb in Tom's direction. "Off his trolley! Out of his tree! Sandwich short of a picnic!" And he laughed his most irritating laugh.

Zed spread out the five notes on the stall, and looked at them one after another. Then, suddenly, he leaned forward to snatch something from between the photograph frames.

"I've got one! A message!" He held up a torn piece of cream paper.

Jamie craned his neck to see. "From J.S.? What does he say?"

The Abacus is proving most valuable. J. S.

Zed read it aloud. "It's signed J.S., like the others. Abacus!" he repeated, holding out the note to show the two boys. "He means the calculator, I suppose. Well, at least he's found something he likes."

"What's an abacus?" Jamie asked.

"A sort of counting gadget, with beads on wires," Zed explained. "Little kids have them sometimes, to help them learn to add and subtract."

"You should get yourself one, Jamie, for school," Tom said, grinning. "So J.S. worked out how to use it, then. Even though he can't have seen one before."

"Clever ghost," said Zed.

Jamie stared at him. "You're not swallowing this ghost idea, too, are you? Loopy, both of you!"

Tom said, "All this bartering he's been doing – or at least leaving things in exchange for what he's taken – it's not because he hasn't got money. It's just that he hasn't got the *right* money. I suppose he'd have guineas and sovereigns, wouldn't he? Not 20p and 50p and pound coins."

"Bats, both of you." Jamie shook his head sadly.

All the time they'd been talking, Bill at the next stall had been keeping up his continuous chant. "CLEMENTINES, PAHND A BAG ... LOVELY RIPE PINEAPPLES, SPECIAL TODAY ... LEEKS,

90p A PAHND ... KIWI FRUIT –" Suddenly he broke off, and Tom heard him exclaim, "Well, I'll be ..."

Tom and Jamie dashed round to see what was happening. Bill and Mary were both staring at an empty space at the front of their stall. Between a box of King Edwards and a box of Granny Smiths, there was a gap on the fake grass.

Mary threw up her arms in disbelief. "A whole box of kiwi fruit just disappeared into thin air!"

Bill scratched his head and screwed up his face. "Both of us standing here! One minute it's here – the next, vanished! I'm going round the twist, Mary! We both are!"

He collapsed into a canvas chair at the back of the stall and took off his cloth cap. Then he looked down at the ground, did a double take and flopped back, fanning himself with his cap.

"Mary," he called. "Am I seeing things, or is there a massive basket of eggs down here?"

Tom couldn't help giving Jamie a triumphant look. "Barmy, am I? Loopy? Round the twist? Well, what's your explanation?"

65

7 Grumpy Gordon

"Here comes Grumpy Gordon," Jamie said.
"What's he doing out of his shop?"

Tom peered round the Indian scarves to look.
Gordon, from Bitz and Bytes, was stumping along
the row, carrying a sturdy cardboard box. He
stopped by Zed's stall.

"Someone was telling me you keep chickens,"
he said to Zed, without so much as a 'hello' or
'how's business?'

Zed looked warily at the box. "*A* chicken," he
said. "Just the one."

"Want another to keep it company?" Gordon
pushed the box across the stall, and Tom heard
something shifting its weight inside. "Don't know
what to do with it, otherwise. Some joker left it in
my shop."

Zed lifted the lid of the box a fraction and
peered in, then opened wider. "This is some

chicken! D'you know what breed it is?" he asked
Gordon.

Tom looked in, and saw a chicken with
magnificent golden plumage, a bright eye that
fixed him with an accusing stare, and thick
feathers that went all the way down to its feet,
like pyjamas.

"Don't ask me." Gordon yawned hugely,
suddenly looking as if he could drop off to sleep
where he stood. "I've just about had enough of
chickens and turkeys, I can tell you. Hardly had a

wink of sleep from last week to this."

"Oh?" Zed prompted.

"You know I've got the flat above the shop? Well, every time I get to sleep, I get woken up by blasted chickens! Cackling, gobbling, scratching, squawking, cock-a-doodle-dooing – you wouldn't believe the noise they make!"

"Where are they?" Zed asked.

Gordon huffed. "Oh, there aren't any *actual* chickens – that's the annoying thing about it. It sounds like the flat's full of them. But the minute I get out of bed to check, it all stops – everything quiet as you like. Till I get back to sleep, that is. It's driving me spare!"

Jamie was staring at Gordon closely. Another one going mental, he was clearly thinking.

"Not just me, either," Gordon went on. "Young chap next door, manager of Quiksnax – when I told him, for a bit of a joke, like, thinking he'd laugh, he said, 'Funny, I had a disturbed night as well, full of dreams about chickens with staring eyes and great big beaks!' Coincidence, or what?"

"Hmm," said Tom.

"But there was at least *one* real chicken," Zed pointed out, with a hand on the box.

"Oh, that one. Behind the counter, that one

was, sitting there quite happy. Someone must have sneaked it in while I wasn't looking. Whoever's playing a joke on me, I wish they'd pick on someone else." He yawned again. "Well, my shop won't run itself. I can leave you this bird, then? Or shall I give it to matey to turn into Quikchik burger?"

"I'll have her," Zed said quickly. "I'd been thinking of getting a friend for Erica – that's my other chicken. Look, you must take something in exchange. Candlestick? Wall hanging? Something nice for your flat?"

"No, thanks very much." Gordon backed away. "I'm happy to get that bird off my hands."

Zed was delighted with Chicken No. 2. As soon as Gordon had gone, he announced that he was going to call her Betty.

"Why Betty?" Tom asked.

"Our other grandmother," Jamie said, grinning.

By the end of the day, Tom felt that he had quite a few clues to follow up. He couldn't wait till next Saturday, now that he had such good leads. As Jamie was so scornful, Tom decided it was time for some research on his own.

After school on Monday, he went to the library behind the town hall, to see if he could find out anything that would throw light on the Mapplesham

Market Mystery. The librarian found him a book all about Mapplesham – a very old book, with black-and-white photographs going back to Victorian times. He sat down at one of the tables and leafed through. The market had originally been a sheep and cattle market. There were pictures showing the square filled with pens, and farmers looking at the animals for sale. The market square hadn't really changed much since then, though most of the shops were different – the signs above the doors said things like 'Gunsmith', 'Apothecary', 'Haberdasher' – but Tom recognised the market cross, the town hall and the patterned brickwork of the post office. And some shops still had the same names: Pearson's Sweets and Bollinger's Books.

Then, turning the page, Tom noticed something that made him stare more closely.

'The Market Square in Victorian Times,' said the caption. What had alerted Tom's attention was the shop in one corner of the square – a big, prosperous-looking grocer's shop.

Chickens, turkeys and pheasants hung outside in rows – some plucked, some still with their feathers on. Eggs were heaped in baskets. The owner stood in the doorway with arms folded, looking out at the market. Tom couldn't read the name above the door, because the branches of a tree hung in the way – a tree that wasn't there now. But he knew where that shop was. Now, it was divided into two: one half was Bitz and Bytes, Gordon's computer shop, and the other was Quiksnax.

Tom bent over the picture to study the man in the doorway. He was a big, sturdy man, filling the door-frame. He wore a long white apron and had his shirtsleeves rolled up. He had a twinkling sort of smile and bushy side whiskers that framed his face, and he looked very pleased with himself and his shop.

J.S.! This must be J.S.! If only he could read the name of the shop, he felt sure it would say 'Joe Sampson', or 'Joshua Smith', or 'John Stubbs'. Finding no more, he went to the desk to ask if there were any more books about the market.

"I'm sure there are," said the helpful librarian, looking at her computer screen. "At least one. Here we are – *Mapplesham Memories*. It's out now, though – due back Saturday. If you like, I'll put it aside for you."

Saturday seemed a very long time to wait, now that Tom felt he was on the trail of J.S. He felt himself tingling on the edge of discovery. If only the borrower of *Mapplesham Memories* remembered to return it! Tom couldn't bear to think of it sitting on someone's bedside table, forgotten, gathering dust, while he fretted with impatience.

By next Saturday there was only a fortnight to go until Christmas, and the market was in festive mood. Carol-singers performed outside the town hall, accompanied by a brass band. The hot dog van sold mince pies and coffee and roasted chestnuts. Coloured lights were draped round all the lamp-posts, to be turned on later when it started to get dark. Bill and Mary's stall was hung with holly and mistletoe, and Brian's stationery table was draped with wrapping paper, gift tags and ribbons. Zed was doing a good trade in candlesticks and some table decorations he'd made with candles, holly and ivy.

Tom had decided to say nothing to Jamie or Zed until he had more hard evidence, but when Jamie went off to get Zed's breakfast, he couldn't keep quiet any longer. He had opened his mouth to say, "I've been doing some research," when Zed spoke first.

"I've been doing some research."

"What?" Tom said, with the weird sense that his own words were coming out of someone else's mouth.

"I said, I've been doing some research," Zed repeated.

"What sort of research?"

"About my new chicken, Betty. I didn't know what sort of chicken she is, so I went into the bookshop and found *The Poultry Keeper's Handbook* and looked her up, and there she was."

"There was Betty?"

"A chicken just like her," said Zed. "She's a Cochin. With that thick plumage, and leg feathers like pyjamas. And a very loud voice, as I've found out early every morning this week.

A Cochin," he said, looking hard at Tom, "is a breed of hen that was very popular around the time of Queen Victoria, because Queen Victoria had some herself."

"Oh," Tom said. "Hmm. Queen Victoria. But I suppose you can still get them nowadays?"

"Yes, I'm sure you can," said Zed. "Just like you can still get a copy of *A Christmas Carol*."

"How much are the candles?" someone called out, and they were both busy with customers until Jamie came back with Zed's tea and peanut butter sandwich and two cans of cola.

"Guess what?" he told them, bursting with news. "Gordon's not here today. Bitz and Bytes is all shut up. He must have had enough of the chicken noises. And the chap in Quiksnax is looking a bit frazzled, as well."

* * * * *

At lunchtime, Tom slipped away to the library.

"Here," said the librarian, handing over a hardback book. "Came back a day early. Hope you find what you want."

Tom sat in a corner seat, trying to devour all the pages at once. The book had been written by an old man who had lived in Mapplesham all his life, from 1860 till after the Second World War. Tom flicked through, skimming – farms, new roads, the railway. At last, reaching a section about local shops, he slowed down to read properly.

A name leapt out of the page at him.

I was very sorry when Josiah Swithinbank's specialist grocery shop closed down, just after the turn of the century. Mr Swithinbank had gone from humble beginnings as a poultry-keeper to run one of the biggest shops in Mapplesham. He rented 1–2 Market Square and ran a thriving shop for several years. Because of his background in chicken rearing, he specialised in poultry, though as he became successful he sold all sorts of other things besides. We always bought our eggs from him, and our Christmas turkey, and he had a wonderful range of sausages, jams, pies, mustards and relishes. He left the town very suddenly in 1899. The owner of the buildings, Ernest Quick, was a wealthy banker, and according to local gossip he threw out Mr Swithinbank, then let the shop to someone else, at a much higher rent. First I knew was Swithinbank's shop had shutters over the doors and windows, and a few weeks later the place reopened as a coffee house. Since then there have been all sorts of comings and goings, but no one's stayed for long.

Got him! Tom's fists clenched in triumph. Josiah Swithinbank, a poultry keeper! That *had* to be J.S., the Mystery Market Visitor. And tricked by Quick! That explained the Quiksnax note about effrontery and throwing down a gauntlet.

Now to tell Zed, and convince Jamie. Even Jamie would have to admit that this was more than coincidence!

8 Comeback

It was so frustrating! Just when Tom felt he was hot on the trail of J.S., it was the end of term, and Tom went away for almost the whole holiday, to stay with his grandparents in Scotland. He liked going there and seeing his Scottish cousins, but it was almost New Year before he went back to the market.

By that time, the Market Mystery seemed to have happened so long ago that he would have thought he'd dreamed it all, if it weren't for J.S.'s messages, all kept carefully by Zed in a wooden box. Jamie, who had helped Zed the Saturday before Christmas, reported that there had been no more strange happenings. "Mind you, we were busy all day. Best day's taking Zed's ever had, so he gave me a bonus. Shame you missed it!"

"So nothing happened, then? No more messages, or bartering?"

"Not that I heard of. Didn't have time to go looking – anyway, it wouldn't have been the same, on my own."

Tom felt despondent, sunk into a post-Christmas slump. The first market after Christmas was always a bit of a let-down. The weather was dreary, wet and cold, and the decorations on the stalls looked tired and soggy. He felt that J.S. had slipped from his grasp like a slippery fish. Jamie would never be convinced unless Josiah Swithinbank walked up to their stall and introduced himself. Even Zed, though impressed by Tom's discoveries in the library, had come to the conclusion that someone had been playing an elaborate joke, pretending to be Josiah Swithinbank. As he pointed out, *any*one could have borrowed *Mapplesham Memories* from the library.

Tom and Jamie fetched Zed's breakfast and came back to find Sadia at the stall, looking at calendars. Zed seemed to be showing her every single picture in every single calendar. There were no customers in sight, least of all ghostly Victorians with quill pens, Cochin hens or leather-bound volumes of Charles Dickens. Nothing was going to happen today, Tom felt sure. Josiah Swithinbank – or whoever was pretending to be him – had finished his fun and games.

"Everyone's still in bed, sleeping off their Christmas binges," Jamie complained. "Else they're at the sales. It was hardly worth coming today. I could be playing with my new computer game if I'd stayed in."

"But it wouldn't be Saturday without the market," Tom said.

Jamie kicked at a squashed tomato that had fallen off Bill's stall and rolled along the ground a few yards before being trodden on. "There's not much point, today. People aren't going to buy Zed's candles and stuff, not just after Christmas. He'll be talking to Sadia for the next two hours, you wait and see."

"Tell you what," Tom suggested, "why don't we do the whole Market Maze? We haven't done it for a few weeks. And backwards," he added. "An extra challenge might add excitement to a dull day."

"You mean walking backwards? Or starting at the end and finishing at the start?"

"I mean the other way round from normal,

dingbat. You can walk backwards, if you want."

Jamie nodded. "All right – might as well. But don't fall into Pet Shop Man's clutches again."

They went to the market cross, their starting point. Tom couldn't help feeling just a bit nervous. Doing the Maze backwards took quite an effort of memory, and there was more risk of being caught today in forbidden places, with fewer shoppers than usual to distract the stallholders' attention.

"Can you remember it, backwards?" he said doubtfully.

"Yeah, course," Jamie said. He was wearing brand new trainers, a Christmas present. Tom thought this was a bit daft, considering how wet and puddly it was today.

They started off along their normal finishing straight, the section from the market cross to the far side of the cheese van. From here, the route jinked away from the market square, swerving into a tiny, low alleyway between Pearson's Sweets and an antique seller's, then turning sharply right into a narrow lane behind two shops. Ahead of you, although you didn't go through it, was a brick archway that led to Church Street, one of the main roads into town. Tom was walking with his hood up and head down against the rain, but looked up when Jamie grabbed his arm.

"See that? That man there? Oh, too slow! Just saw him through the arch."

"So?"

"He's big, and I mean big –" Jamie mimed with puffed-up chest and spread shoulders, "and wearing this weird fancy dress. Like, a big cape made of tweedy stuff, and a bowler hat, and trousers tucked into those legging things – what d'you call them?"

"Gaiters?" Tom ventured.

"Gaiters, and he had a walking stick. D'you reckon it was him? Mystery Man himself?"

"Stop winding me up!" Tom waggled his head so that rain dripped from the front of his hood.

All that could be seen was the steady flow of traffic towards the market square one-way system. Tyres splashed on the wet road.

"I'm not! Quick, let's catch him up!" Jamie set off at a fast pace, Tom following – dodging past the Lotus Moon Chinese Restaurant's dustbins. Reaching the pavement, Tom looked to his right.

"Okay, so where is he?"

"Look! There!" Jamie pointed, and Tom glimpsed the big, burly figure striding purposefully into the market, his tweed cape swinging as he strode. Excitement quickened. No ordinary person came to the market dressed like that!

"Come on!" Jamie ordered. "We'll head him off – get a better look. Told you it was only someone in fancy dress! Ghost in gaiters – I don't think so!"

He dashed on, Tom in pursuit, splashing through puddles. Abandoning the maze route, they darted between boxes of tea towels and tea cosies, ducked under a low flap of awning, straight on past pottery and dried flowers – nearly crashing into a spiky huddle of umbrellas where a group of shoppers had stopped to chat – and took a sharp left turn, ducking past the flower stall, into the hidden corner stacked with boxes of carnations wrapped in cellophane. There was just room for both boys to fit in, although Tom was balanced awkwardly with one foot on a crate. He lifted a corner of awning, and water dripped into his sleeve and down his arm.

"He's coming!" Jamie hissed. "Don't let him see us."

Tom couldn't see all of the strange man, but what he could see was unmistakable. His feet and legs advanced down the aisle, framed by the swinging cape and the walking stick: sturdy legs in thick woollen trousers. Brown boots, polished to a high shine. Gaiters of some sort of canvas material, buttoned at the sides. The cape was of thick, heavy brown tweed, and the knobbly walking stick was capped in metal. As the man passed the hiding place, Tom smelled damp wool, carbolic soap, and something pungent that could be mothballs.

"Nice outfit," said Jamie. "He's probably collecting money for the hospital, or something like that. He'll get out a money tin in a minute."

"No!" Tom whispered back. "This is the real J.S. – I'm sure it is!"

"Oh yeah, how d'you make that out?" Jamie shifted his weight, almost knocking over the flower box. "If he's your actual ghost, how come he's walking about in full view, when he's always been the Invisible Man before?"

"Don't know," Tom said, "but it is him, I know it is! Look, he'll go round by the burger van, won't he? If we get there first, we'll have a good look at him."

Jamie stared. "How do you *know* he'll go round by the van?"

"'Cos he's heading for his shop, course –" Tom began, when an angry voice behind made him jump.

"Oi! Blooming kids! What you up to, eh?"

The flower stall owner loomed into the gap. Tom didn't feel like staying to explain. A huge hand stretched out to grab him, with fingers like the claws on a JCB excavator. Taking a deep breath, Tom dashed underneath the man's grabbing arm.

They were heading in the wrong direction, but with Flower Stall Man blocking the entrance there was only one choice – the central tunnel.

They scrambled over Brian's boxes of books, past fish and knitting, and safely through the treacherous reaches of the pet stall (Tom sticking his tongue out at Pet Shop Man's back). They burst out into the open, to the surprise of a dog sitting there scratching itself, then doubled back past Sadia's fashions, Mr Miserable's toys, and Marion's sweets. Here, Tom stood panting, facing the burger van. He gazed around while Jamie caught up.

Doug and Derek, the elderly bikers, were standing by the burger van, regardless of the rain, drinking coffee. As Tom watched, Doug pointed at something, and Derek turned to stare. J.S. must have taken a diversion to look at the cheese van, as he was now walking towards them, twirling his stick. Tom saw that he had apple-red cheeks and a magnificent set of side-whiskers.

Doug and Derek stared, mouths frozen in amazed 'O's, and at the same time J.S. turned to

his left and saw them.
For a second their
expressions matched
exactly, as J.S. stopped
dead to stare at
Doug's and Derek's
skinny, black leather
outfits, skull badges
and lank, rain-soaked,
grey hair. Clearly, none
of J.S.'s previous visits had
brought him into contact with Mapplesham's
Hell's Grandads.

Tom giggled, then realised that J.S. was heading
towards him and Jamie.

They stood back against the van. J.S. continued
his progress. For a second, he looked straight at
Tom, and Tom looked at him – looked into the
big, whiskered face of Josiah Swithinbank, the
face he'd seen in the photograph. J.S. raised his
bowler hat as he passed, then crossed the
pavement and headed towards the computer shop.

Except that it wasn't a computer shop any
more. Staring, Tom saw that the shop had been
completely renovated since he'd last seen it. The
computers were gone, and the plate glass front
replaced with green tiles and panes of bottle-end

glass. The Bitz and Bytes name had gone, replaced by a painted sign above the door:

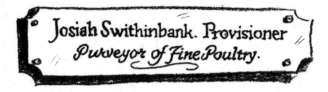

Josiah Swithinbank. Provisioner
Purveyor of Fine Poultry.

"Josiah Swithinbank!" Tom whispered to Jamie. "Now tell me it's not him!"

Josiah Swithinbank reached into his trouser pocket and took out a large, shiny key. He opened the shop door and went inside.

"He's got his old shop back!" Tom said. "He's waited all this time!"

"Oh, come on!" Jamie gave Tom one of his 'you're barmy' looks. "There's an obvious explanation, isn't there? Gordon got fed up and packed in his shop – probably moved somewhere bigger. And this bloke's taken over. A lot of people like these old-fashioned-looking shops, don't they? I expect he thinks it's a nice idea to dress up old-fashioned, as well."

"What about all the messages he left?" Tom protested. "All the things that came and went without anyone noticing? I bet he was doing market research! Checking out the stalls, waiting for his moment to make a comeback! It's him, I know it is – I've seen his photo!"

But he'd never convince Jamie. If Josiah Swithinbank was a ghost, he was a very robust, healthy-looking, well-fed, flesh-and-blood ghost.

"If you're still trying to tell me that's your actual Josiah Swithinbank from a hundred years ago," Jamie said, "then you really are out of your tree. If he's a ghost, I'm Donald Duck."

"*Waaak, waaak, waaak,*" Tom quacked, startling a

passing lady who raised her umbrella to peer at him suspiciously. "Okay then, Donald. Let's have a look inside, shall we?"

Jamie frowned. "What, go in there? Inside the shop?"

Inside, Mr Swithinbank was putting up a 'Grand Opening' sign in the window.

"Not scared, are you?"

"As if!" Jamie scoffed.

They crossed the road and hesitated in Josiah Swithinbank's doorway. The inside of the shop had been completely refitted. There was a large

marble counter, loaded with baskets of brown and speckled eggs, each clutch nestling in a bed of straw. The back wall was hung with plump, plucked chickens and turkeys. The shelves were stacked with big round cheeses, jars of pickles and chutneys, and stone mustard jars. There was a large set of scales, with weights, standing next to Zed's calculator. The floor was sprinkled with sawdust, and everything was spotlessly clean. Delicious smells wafted out into the street – mulled wine, roasting chestnuts and hot, herb-filled sausages.

"Mmmm!" went Jamie, twitching his nose like a rabbit's. "Is he giving away free samples?"

"Quiksnax next door had better watch out," Tom muttered. "I bet he's got plans to take over both halves of his old shop. Quick was the name of the bloke that cheated him! That's why he left that message about gauntlets."

By now they weren't the only ones to take an interest in the newcomer to the market square. Several other people had drifted over, drawn by the new window and the intoxicating smells, while next door Quiksnax was completely empty, the manager poking his head out of the door to see what was going on.

"Go on, if you're going." Jamie gave Tom a shove, and they both stepped inside.

On the counter stood a cardboard notice, in handwriting Tom knew well.

Try our original range of chutneys and relishes. Prepared with the finest exotic fruits from the Southern Hemisphere.

Tom looked more closely. The counter was stacked with jars.

Each had a patterned fabric cover, tied with ribbon, and each jar had been labelled by hand.

"Kiwi Fruit Chutney," Tom read. "Kiwi Fruit

Gentleman's Relish, Kiwi Fruit Curd and Kiwi Fruit Marmalade."

Tom looked up. Josiah Swithinbank was standing behind the counter in a long white apron, arms folded, smiling behind his bushy side-whiskers and looking very pleased with himself.

Tom caught his eye, and just for a second he almost imagined that Josiah Swithinbank winked.